I REMEMBER ABBU

I REMEMBER
ABBU

HUMAYUN AZAD

Translated by Arunava Sinha
Interior Illustrations by Sabyasachi Mistry

Text copyright © 1989 & 2000 by Humayun Azad
Translation copyright © 2019 by Arunava Sinha
All rights reserved.

Previously published as *Abbu k mone pore* by Bangladesh Shisu Academy in Bangladesh in 1989 and by Agamee Prakashani in Bangladesh in 2000. Translated from Bengali by Arunava Sinha. First published in English by AmazonCrossing in 2019.

Published by AmazonCrossing, Seattle

www.apub.com

Amazon, the Amazon logo, and AmazonCrossing are trademarks of Amazon.com, Inc., or its affiliates.

ISBN-13: 9781542042420
ISBN-10: 1542042429

Cover design by Micaela Alcaino

Interior illustrations by Sabyasachi Mistry

Printed in the United States of America

I REMEMBER ABBU

FOREWORD

I was deeply shaken when I first read this book in my younger years and spent many sleepless nights with an intense pain. This book moved my young heart. I felt alone on earth after losing my father all those years ago. This thought—that my dad was gone forever, the very truth that he was no longer there for me whenever I needed him the most—used to eat me up inside constantly and drove me to tears. It wasn't a pleasant feeling.

Having read this book, I learned about Bangladesh's independence war, our freedom fighters; I learned about the collaborators and the ruthlessness of the Pakistani army; I became familiar with the environment and the circumstances during the war of 1971; and most importantly I realized my own dreams and the relationship between a father and his son. For the first time in my young life, this book taught me the sheer value and importance of living in a free country. I was very young—my thought process was simple—and I was not even aware, to tell you the truth, that the author of this book was the father of my own when I first read it. I vividly recall how I often used to run to my dad for comfort because I knew I could always rest easily on his shoulders. My dad was my rock.

I wasn't fortunate enough to enjoy my father's unconditional love and his unwavering support for me and for my siblings for a very long period of time, however. It was cut short abruptly. I remember, when I was slowly getting to know my surroundings—my world, my then-world of thirteen years, in 2004—I witnessed the bloodied body of my father when he was attacked by that very force that did not want to see my beloved Bangladesh as an independent country, forever free from the atrocities of Pakistan, that evil force that could not fathom why we should have our own flag and that despised my beloved language, Bengali, so rich in texture along with its literature, which my father loved so dearly. In the year of 2004, on February 27, my father was brutally attacked by these Islamic zealots who intended to silence him by killing him once and for all. My father's lifeless body was discovered later that year in Munich, Germany, in a flat where he had arrived just days earlier to conduct research on the German poet Heinrich Heine. My father, a professor at the University of Dhaka, was invited by PEN International at the time.

In the book, the father never did return, but the country was liberated. Every time there's a knock on the door, there is someone coming home by the end of the day; but just like the fictional character in the book, my father will never come home—I know this well. I miss my dad; he believed that writers should be able to speak their minds freely and he was right, we all know. I, too, believe in this—my exiled life today is self-explanatory.

I often wonder now, did we achieve our independence in a true sense? Or is our independence only written in a mere constitution or in some heartwarming piece of literature? If we did get our freedom to speak freely, why was my father attacked so brutally? Why am I now living in exile thousands of miles away from my beloved country?

I have always believed in good human nature.

I know and I will always believe that people are basically good.

On this note, I present this book to you with gratitude.

Ananya Azad
Hamburg, Germany
December 2, 2018

Anyone who lived in the country today named Bangladesh before August 14–15, 1947, has actually lived in three countries. Anyone who was born after that, but lived there before March 26, 1971, has lived in two countries.

The land of Bangladesh was a part of India, ruled at different times by local kings, central emperors, and the British, up until August 14–15, 1947. On those days, two countries became independent of British rule. One was India, and the other was the newly born country of Pakistan, carved out of India in an act of partition by the British, ostensibly to create a separate homeland for Muslims.

Pakistan came into being in two blocks—West and East—that were separated by more than thirteen hundred miles and shared only a religion, Islam. East Pakistan had more in common with the undivided state of Bengal in prepartitioned India than it did with West Pakistan.

Perhaps the greatest difference was language. While the official language of West Pakistan was Urdu—its citizens also spoke local tongues like Punjabi and Sindhi—the language of East Pakistan was Bangla, widely known as Bengali.

This proved a bone of contention as early as 1948, barely a year after Pakistan was born. When the West Pakistan–based government made Urdu the sole national language, the language movement, which pressed for recognition of Bangla, began.

On February 21, 1952, there was a protest by students and political activists in Dhaka, the principal city of East Pakistan (and now the capital of Bangladesh). In a horrific show of power, the police attacked demonstrators and killed a number of students. That was the symbolic beginning of a widespread movement that escalated later into a full-fledged liberation war.

Relations between East and West Pakistan deteriorated, with things coming to a head in 1970. In that year, Sheikh Mujibur Rahman, a Bengali politician from East Pakistan, led his party, the Awami League, to victory in the very first democratic election held in Pakistan since the advent of military rule in 1958. However, the military junta refused to allow Mujibur Rahman to assume power, which prompted the freedom movement to accelerate.

A "liberation army" sprang into existence, largely comprising young civilians. There were open and covert battles with the military in Dhaka and across East Pakistan, with the army gradually being put on the defensive. Seeing an opportunity, the Indian government, whose own relations with Pakistan had worsened, offered military help to the freedom movement. A full-fledged war began between Pakistan and India, and the former finally surrendered in December 1971.

Even before this, under the leadership of Mujibur Rahman, East Pakistan declared its independence, and March 26, 1971, is considered the official date on which the new nation of Bangladesh came into existence. The name of the country came from Bangla, the language, and *desh*, the Bangla word for country or nation. The identity of the new country was, thus, explicitly built around the language.

In 1999, UNESCO acknowledged the language movement by designating the date International Mother Language Day.

The plight of the people of Bangladesh and their liberation war attracted international attention, and relief poured in from all over the world. Among the fund-raising events organized was the famous Concert for Bangladesh on August

1, 1971, at Madison Square Garden in New York City, put together by former Beatles star George Harrison and Indian sitar player Ravi Shankar. In an album released the next year, *Come from the Shadows*, folk musician Joan Baez sang movingly of a later 1971 massacre of students in Bangladesh.

Arunava Sinha
2018

To those young people
Who have grown up with grief in their
hearts
Who will grow up with grief in their
hearts
Who exist in grief
Who will exist in grief
Within whose hearts is suspended
A single drop of water
Which will never fall
Those who have grown up
But are still lonely
For they have lost something of theirs
Perhaps their heart
Perhaps the world
Perhaps the life
Which no one gave them
Which no one can give them

I Remember / Don't Remember Abbu

I don't remember Abbu. I don't exactly know what an abbu is like. I don't know what an abbu's face is like, what his lips are like, how they look when kissing my cheek, how he combs his hair, which side he parts it on, how he rings the doorbell, what kind of sound the doorbell makes or for how long, whether it plays the tune "I've come back to you, come back to you." I don't know any of these things about my father.

I haven't seen Abbu for sixteen years. I won't see Abbu for sixteen hundred years. Had I seen my abbu before those sixteen years, my ab-bu? I don't remember Abbu. There was a very significant year. It was called seventy-one. I was four then. How strange to think I saw Abbu at one. Even at two. And three. I'm shocked when I think about it, and I remember Abbu so much then. Because I don't remember Abbu.

What was my abbu like? Was he fat? No. Was he thin? No. Was he very tall? Very short? No. Was he extremely fair? Exceptionally dark? No. My abbu was exactly the way my abbu was. I don't remember Abbu.

I do know Abbu had long hair. His ears were covered by his curls, and he wore glasses. Thick dark frames. And he never wore shoes; he wore sandals. People look kind of like policemen when they don't wear shoes, and they look kind of ordinary when they don't wear glasses. So, my abbu never looked like a policeman. My abbu looked exactly as extraordinary as he was.

For sixteen years, I've been talking to Abbu. My friends are frightened of their abbus, staying out of their way. They slip out of their homes. When they return, they hesitate for a long time before fearfully ringing the doorbell. I'm not afraid of my abbu. I run into him all the time. When I'm going out this door. When I'm going out that door. When I'm coming back. We stand side by side on the balcony. When I hail a rickshaw, I see Abbu smiling at me from the balcony.

"I'm going now, Abbu," I say.

"Be careful in that rickshaw," he says, waving.

"Don't worry," I say. "I'm more careful than you."

He waves again.

The rickshaw starts moving, and Abbu's smile hangs in the air behind me.

But before long, I see Abbu coming toward me in another rickshaw. I wave in passing, and he waves back. No one's abbu spreads themselves everywhere like my abbu does. No one's abbu smiles at everyone or hovers nearby all the time.

I remember Abbu. I don't remember Abbu.

The Face of a Rose

I have never looked closely at a rose, Abbu wrote in his diary. *But her face reminded me of a rose.* Abbu wrote this in his diary on the night I was born.

My eyelids were puffy. My eyes were barely visible. Abbu wrote, *If she has stars in her eyes, they are even more distant than the stars in the sky.* Did I arrive in the land of Bangla with my eyes closed? Did I arrive on Earth with my eyes closed?

It was a fine day to arrive on the planet. Abbu wrote, *Is everyone against her? Have people gone mad because she is coming? But she has decided she is coming. Who can stop her? Who can stop a human?*

Abbu had great faith in humans. And in the human who was on her way.

A demon had occupied the country. And it brought smaller demons with it. And with them, even smaller demons. They had a stack of weapons. Weapons were hooked to each of their claws. A war between humans and demons had begun all over the land.

Abbu wrote, *The map of our land looks like a mangled boot worn by a demon. Every monster has come to trample us.* The country was called East Pakistan at the time, but Abbu only called it Eastern Bangla.

It wasn't because I was about to arrive, but to get rid of the demons, that the people of the land, those millions of princes, had called a general strike, a *hartal*. What a lovely word, "hartal."

I arrived on a boat with flying sails signaling a hartal, skimming the surface of a deserted avenue like a river. The city had been emptied out on one side, and on the other, the air was thick with people and their voices. Police cars went back and forth. I was coming, which was why everyone in Dhaka, and in the village outside Dhaka, and in the small town beyond the village, and in all the villages beyond the small town, was dressed up as a revolutionary.

How beautiful Abbu's handwriting is in his diary.

He had quaked all day, just like the city, and my ammu had been lying on a bed in the clinic, holding me in the heart that lies within the heart. I arrived in a Bangla where the houses and trees had prepared for the war between demons and humans, and the clinic had turned into the place where people were born.

I was born in an earthen hut, amidst the smell of the soil, amidst the fragrance of mango wood and smoke, wrote Abbu. *And she is being born in a dirty clinic, amidst the smell of disinfectants and medicine. I was born in May, when sheaves of grain from the banks of Arial Lake were spilling out of the house and into our front yard, which was caked with cow dung set out to dry. And she is arriving in the middle of a hartal in August.*

It was evening then. An anxious Abbu kept climbing up to the third floor of the clinic and then back down to the road to wait. A procession of people with flaming torches passed him. Once again, Abbu climbed to the third floor, then climbed down. Only two of the doctors had made it to the clinic. The country, the city, the clinic, and Abbu were all ensnared in the tension of the moment.

Abbu climbed to the third floor again around eleven that night.

The nurse told him, "Come, your child is here."

I had been laid out on a tray. I was curled up, my eyes shut. Abbu was racing toward me in delight when a woman, a doctor, stopped him.

"Why have you come here?" she shouted angrily.

"To see her," Abbu said.

"Go away; you don't need to see her," the doctor roared. "Don't you know you're not supposed to go near a newborn baby?"

Abbu was sent away.

I barely laid eyes on her, he wrote. *Humans are not supposed to go near humans. Abbu is not supposed to go near his newborn. Must a father and a mother be separated from their child from the moment of birth?*

I have never looked closely at a rose, Abbu wrote when he got home after the midnight curfew. *But her face reminded me of a rose.*

Cow dung smells far sweeter than antiseptic, Abbu wrote. *I will bring her home early tomorrow morning. Not for another day will I let her stay with the antiseptic or with doctors whose words sting more than antiseptic. I won't let my rose drown in a pool of antiseptic.*

Thou, Her Highness, Genius, and Fool

"How art thou?" This was the first thing Abbu said after taking me in his arms. Then he said, "What is thy command?"

I would have been very happy had I understood him. "Thou"? For a baby like me? It's been so long since anyone addressed me as "thou." I am tired of being referred to as "you." I long to hear "thou."

Everywhere I look, people are older than I am. There's no chance they'll show me respect. I'm the one who has to speak deferentially.

How wonderful it is to be addressed as "thou." It makes me so happy to think Abbu thought me worthy of respect from the very day I was born.

"Oh my, 'thou,'" Ammu had laughed.

"She deserves something even greater," Abbu had said. "After all, she's a human being from the future."

Abbu wrote, *"You" does not suit her. "Your" does not suit her.*

Abbu wrote, *She needs a new pronoun. A new pronoun for a new person.*

As soon as he got home, Abbu would ask, "Where is Her Highness?"

"Thou," and now "Her Highness." Everyone at home knew "Her Highness" referred to me. To little me. I doubt anyone in the family had ever been referred to that way.

Abbu also used to call me a genius. But geniuses are great men and women. Geniuses write fat books. I had barely ripped a single page from a book by then. Geniuses break with tradition. I had only managed to break a cup. Ammu didn't let me break any more. Still, I was a genius to Abbu.

"What is the genius doing?" Abbu would ask.

I was busy with a shoe. I was keen on tasting a shoe.

I had not even managed to learn the language by then. I didn't need language. It didn't befit geniuses like me to talk. It befitted me only to smile and to pout. Geniuses are reticent. I was a supreme genius, which meant emitting a single sound or two was sufficient. From Abbu's diary, I learned that each of my sounds had thousands of meanings. Apparently, my smile contained more elusive wisdom than had been captured in all the books on all the shelves.

No sooner did I begin walking than I earned a new title. Abbu began to address me as "fool."

"Where has thou vanished, fool?"

"Canst thou come here, fool?"

"Climbeth thou on my shoulder, fool."

The word "fool" hung in the air all the time. What a sweet word "fool" was when it came from Abbu's lips. At a time when I did not know how to talk. At a time when I felt no need to talk. I've seen photographs of myself at that age. When I cried, I really did look like an utter fool.

Even now, I can hear Abbu calling me from a distance sometimes: "Fool."

"Abbu," I respond in silence.

Again, I can hear him call me: "Fool."

Only an echo sounds from the distance.

Can't Talk, Can Tell

Abbu's slippers are missing. The pair of red-white-green slippers cannot be found in the spot where Abbu always nudges them with his feet after putting on his sandals. They're not in the living room, or outside the kitchen, or beneath the clothes rack. The maid can't find them. Ammu cannot find them in the fridge.

I know slippers are for feet. That doesn't mean they can walk.

"Where are my slippers, Fazila?" Abbu is shouting.

"My slippers are missing," he's telling Ammu.

Abbu is upset. He gets angry if he can't find his slippers when he comes home. His sandals feel hot on his feet.

Abbu considers me a complete fool. Otherwise, he could have asked me. I was home too. But I couldn't talk yet. I tottered around from one room to another. I didn't like the clothes being arranged neatly on the rack, so I pulled them down to the floor and spread them out. Clothes spread out on the floor are so lovely. I liked putting on large shoes. Wearing the left shoe on the right foot was even more fun. Why does everyone put the left shoe on the left foot?

Since I couldn't talk, Abbu and Ammu assumed I couldn't tell things apart from one another. I was small, but I was a human. Does not being able to talk mean you don't know what's what? Didn't Abbu know the sky even when he himself couldn't speak? Doesn't that cat sitting there know me?

Abbu is annoyed. He's sitting in the living room. I feel sorry for him.

Putting my hands inside the slippers, I enter the living room, saying, "Oi, oi."

Abbu jumps in joy.

I just keep saying, "Oi, oi."

Back then, I considered these little words my entire vocabulary.

Dancing with joy, Abbu picks me up in his arms. "How didst thou know my slippers were missing, fool? How didst thou know, fool? How didst thou, fool?"

A human is a human from the very first day, Abbu had written.

Even as a baby, I got excited whenever that thing sitting on the table near the front door rang. Lying in bed, I'd say, "Allo, allo" to myself. When the doorbell rang, I'd shake in excitement. I knew only too well what that sound was saying. "I'm here, I'm here."

There was something else I liked very much. By now, I had learned to say several words. Every morning, the newspaper would slide beneath our door with a rustle. Sometimes, Fazila would run to hand it to Abbu. On other days, Abbu himself would wait for it by the door. He seemed to be annoyed when it was late, sliding under the door with a rustle. Nowadays, I'm irritated too. I used to wonder, *Where does the newspaper come from? Why does it come only once each day, in the morning? What's in it?*

Picking it up, Abbu would tell Ammu, "Here, ten dead today as well."

"Here, thirty dead today as well," he would say, and start looking sad. I thought all the newspaper did was tell us how many people had died. Everyone had to read about death as soon as they woke up in the morning. At least, that was what Abbu did every day. Then he went out.

I wanted to read about people dying too. What did dying mean? I had already begun to grasp that dying was very bad.

I wanted to take the paper to Abbu. I would loiter by the door every morning. But that Fazila! Whenever there was a rustling sound, she would run with it to Abbu. I couldn't run as quickly as she could. But that one day, it was so wonderful. Fazila had gone out when I heard the rustling sound. I waddled to Abbu with the newspaper and asked him, "Who die totay, Abbu?"

Startled, Abbu told Ammu, "Listen to what the fool is saying; listen to the fool!"

Ammu was astonished too. And I was passed from Abbu's arms to Ammu's to Abbu's to Ammu's.

Of course, I realized at once that deaths are part of the daily news in this country. I had no trouble understanding. Now I read of the deaths every morning on Abbu's behalf.

Abbu had written, *How does she understand this? She has never asked. She has concluded from our conversation that the news of death arrives through the newspaper every morning. Bus accidents, capsized launches, collapsed buildings, people dying like rats. She is obviously a human. Small, but a human.*

By then, I had grown a little older. I could say a lot of words. "Gaas" for "glass," "teevishun" for "television," "lice" for "rice." I adored teevishun.

I used to watch television with Abbu in the evening. Abbu would sit with a book, and I would perch in his lap or by his side. How did so many people get into that box? Why couldn't I get in too? Watching television was wonderful, but I loved what happened when it was switched on or switched off. Abbu would fix a wire to the wall, and then press something in front of the television. At once, a picture would appear. I wanted to fix the wire to the wall and press whatever it was he pressed, but I never managed to. When he didn't like the television, Abbu would press that thing again and pull the wire out, and the teevishun would shut down.

One day, Abbu had gone to the bedroom, leaving me on the sofa. He began talking to Ammu. I was watching television. Abbu would be back soon. I wanted to shut the television down. I pulled the wire out and went to Abbu and Ammu in the bedroom.

"Hate teevishun," I told them.

Abbu laughed. "What's the matter, aged one?"

Then he exclaimed, "Why can't I hear the TV?"

Abbu ran to the living room. He found the television off, the wire pulled out.

Abbu was jumping in excitement. He was frightened too. He told Ammu, "Go see—the fool has pulled the wire out. She has learned just by watching me."

I was laughing happily in Ammu's arms.

I didn't want to pull the wire out. I wanted to press that thing in front to turn it off. But I couldn't reach that high. So, I pulled the wire out. After this, Abbu fixed things so that I couldn't get to the wire. The fun of watching television was gone.

One particular incident from that time made Abbu very happy.

It was when I stood up on my own, without holding on to anything. Like Abbu, I, too, look for significance in everything now. No incident is unimportant; everything holds some significance. Just as our words have meanings, and then meanings beyond those meanings, so, too, do incidents have meanings, and then meanings beyond meanings. Take the electrical wires wound around one another next to our house, two or three of which hung loose. They have a significance. My being able to stand on my own was very significant for Abbu.

One evening, I tried to stand up. I needed to stand up.

Crawling wasn't enough. Standing was necessary.

And then when you can stand, standing isn't enough. You have to walk.

When you know how to walk, walking isn't everything. You have to run.

Now that I had crawled for a long time, I felt the urge to stand up. Abbu and Ammu were in the living room. I tried to stand up in front of them.

The first time I tried, I fell. But I couldn't afford to fall.

Beads of perspiration gathered on my cheeks and nose. I lurched on unsteady feet. The weight of all mankind was upon me. As though I were trying to stand up on behalf of the entire human race.

Once again, I tried to stand upright. I forgot the perspiration. I forgot the small world. I forgot the tilting floor. I stood.

My blood tingled in joy. I clapped, as though applauding the achievement of humanity.

Abbu clapped and hoisted me on his shoulder. Ammu clapped, dancing.

One Afternoon

One particular afternoon was blue like a sky I'd never seen. I remember some things about it; I don't remember some other things about it.

Like Abbu's face, I remember a part of it, and I don't remember the other part. I'd been somewhere that afternoon. I don't remember any of it. All I remember is that an afternoon came that comes only once. It doesn't come again. I was toddling from this room to that, from that room to this. I was going up to the door, saying, "Ou, ou."

I loved going out. Feeling the breeze out there.

"Want to go out, fool?" asked Abbu.

"Ou," I said.

Abbu made me put on red shoes. A red frock. He combed my hair. We went outside. Where was that outside? Even today, I want to go there.

Take me to that outside, Abbu.

I hadn't imagined the outside was so huge. I had been to my *khala*'s house earlier with Ammu. My aunt's house. But Ammu used to wrap me in her sari. And it's possible Ammu didn't even take the outside route to Khala's house. Maybe she took a tunnel or something. Ammu probably didn't know what the outside was like. She still doesn't. Although Ammu works in an office, goes shopping, goes to Khala's house too.

Abbu knew what the outside was like. Abbu had a close friendship with the outside. Where had he taken me? All I remember is that we went into a field.

"Those two are fairies," Abbu told me.

"Failees," I said.

The fairies turned to look at me. Their clothes were redder than mine; their saris were flying in the wind. The moon and the stars were glittering on their cheeks. They gave me a flower.

"Will you come with us?" the fairies asked.

I agreed. One of the fairies flew up in the air with me perched on her wing. The other fairy began to dance. She sped through the wind, dancing; I can still see her soaring through the blue, dancing.

Their names were Monimala or Muktomala or something like that. Or it's possible they had no names. Maybe I'm just imagining the names now.

Abbu was whooshing behind us on a ship.

An enormous orange was dangling near my hand. I tried to pluck it.

"Is there an orange moon too?" I think I said.

"There's even a blue moon," I think the fairy said. "Want to see?"

Before my eyes, there was the blue, and I also saw a blue moon and a green moon and a yellow moon. There were moons everywhere. Could there possibly be so many moons in the sky?

The fairies had set me down on the back of a green fish. It swam off through the air, spraying its color everywhere. The fish flew through blue-green water with me on its back.

Abbu was rushing behind us on a blue ship.

I met a tree. I had never met a tree before.

"I'm a tree," the tree told me. "I stand beneath the sky."

"How happy you must be," I may have said.

I met a seashell.

"I'm a seashell," the seashell told me.

"A seashell? I've never seen you before," I may have said.

I met a bird.

"I'm a bird," the bird told me.

"I'm so happy now that I've seen you," I may have said.

23

"Come, let's go back home," Abbu said.

We turned back homeward. That was the one time I went outside. An outside like the outside, an outside with no inside. An outside where everything is out there. I returned home with Abbu, carrying with me the scent of the bird and the green of the grass and the dance of the fairy and the smell of the fish.

I had gone outside. Even today, I feel like going outside with Abbu.

All Those Difficult Words

"Well, aged one?" Abbu had said.

Ged-one, I had replied in my head.

I did not understand who a "ged-one" was. But as soon as I heard the word, I had an image of someone like Dadu, my ancient grandfather. The word always seems very old—a word that finds it painful to stand erect, a word that needs to be massaged all day.

From that day, I developed a liking for difficult words.

Ammu always referred to me as a boy. "My boy," she told her friends when she met them.

"My son," Abbu would say, pointing me out to his friend.

"Mai-zon." How wonderful it felt to hear it. It made me think I was male. Whenever someone says "boy," it makes me feel like a boy. Hearing the word "son" makes me feel like I'm standing next to Abbu.

"Say 'mai-zon,'" I told Abbu.

"Oh my, you can say that too?" a pleased Abbu asked.

Whenever he spoke, I'd tell him, "Say a big word, Abbu."

"What word?" Abbu would ask.

"Red," I'd say.

"Incarnadine," Abbu would say.

Everything would turn utterly red at once. "Incarnadine" is so much redder than red.

"Incarnadine" makes me picture the rising sun. Roses. Ammu's cheeks. Whereas "red" only makes me think of putting on my shoes.

"Abbu, flowers," I'd say.

"Blossoms," Abbu would respond.

My heart would ring with blossoms, blossoms, blossoms, blossoms, blossoms . . . I could see the garden, with blossoms on every branch. I couldn't get enough of them.

"Food," I'd say.

"Victuals," Abbu would respond.

"Evening," I'd say.

"Gloaming," Abbu would respond.

"Fish," I'd say.

"Piscis," Abbu would respond.

I would be astonished. There was a big word for everything. I used to love the big words.

"Want victuals," I told Ammu one day.

Ammu's eyes widened. "What! Victuals? Where did you learn that?"

I chuckled. "Ammu fagerbasted."

I had heard Abbu say it. I can pronounce "flabbergasted" now. But back then, I would murmur all the time, "Fagerbasted, fagerbasted, fagerbasted."

Whenever anyone spoke, I said, "Fagerbasted."

I remember all the big words.

I love all the big words.

The Kittens

One day, a pair of kittens came into our house. One was milky white, dazzling moonlight. I wanted to hug it all the time. Such a beautiful cry: "Miaow!" The other was black and white. They danced into the house.

"Miaow, miaow," they said as soon as they came in.

I looked at them joyfully. There was no one younger than me at home. My heart was filled with happiness now that there were not one but two others younger than me. We didn't have a tiger or an elephant or even a stupid cow at home. But the arrival of the two kittens made up for all that. I pulled out a handful of the white kitten's fur.

Within minutes, the kittens were lost in play. They rolled over each other. All they did was roll. I crawled toward them.

"Don't go near them; you'll catch something," said Ammu.

She dragged me away.

Abbu was also very happy about the arrival of the kittens. How much could he play with me alone? How many times could he hoist me on his shoulder, or lie back in bed and balance me on his knees, or pinch my cheeks?

I couldn't jump or leap like them. I could only shout, "Oi, oi!" in excitement when the kittens did somersaults.

Abbu would roll paper balls for them to play with, and the kittens would turn into tigers. As though it were not a paper ball but a deer that had lost its way and blundered into their path.

They would lie in ambush. Then they would extend one paw before pouncing on the paper ball to sink their claws into it. But they wouldn't try to eat it immediately. Instead, they would hold it with their paws.

Then they would start toying with the prey.

They turned our home into the Sundarbans forests. Abbu would throw paper balls continuously, and they would pounce on them. One hunt followed another in quick succession, and they pounced and pounced and pounced. They couldn't stop pouncing with so many targets around them.

"Oi, oi!" I would shout from Abbu's arms.

I wanted to pounce too.

I wished I could be a milky-white kitten. Who didn't have to crawl. Who was not afraid of catching something. Who didn't have to drink milk from a bottle.

Abbu grew very fond of the kittens. He would toss them up in the air, and they would land perfectly on their feet.

I had learned to walk. And to talk. The kittens had grown.

The white kitten refused to leave home. The black-and-white kitten refused to come home. Once, Abbu tied it up with a length of rope. Still, he couldn't keep it at home.

"A kitten isn't a cow," Ammu said. "You can't tether it."

"But it refuses to stay at home," Abbu said.

"Lefuse home," I said.

Ammu set the black-and-white one loose. It went out. It didn't come back.

The white one stayed. One day, I heard several kittens mewing. Where were they? Beneath our bed.

The white kitten carried them from one spot to another in its mouth. Then from the second spot back to the first.

It set them next to me. Beneath my pillow. On my bottle.

Dadu said, "She'll catch something. Get rid of the kittens."

Abbu was sad.

Something happened that afternoon. A tomcat came into the house and pounced on one of the kittens. Abbu ran to chase him away. But the kitten collapsed. The tomcat had bitten it on the head. The skin had come off. It couldn't get up. Abbu put some medicine on its head. But it didn't survive.

Abbu asked for all the doors to be locked so that the tomcat couldn't get in. All tomcats did was kill kittens.

The tomcat couldn't get back in after that. But there was a crisis.

I loved the new kittens. Ammu came out of the kitchen to find me holding them. Dadu found me kissing one of them. Abbu found their fur in my mouth.

"Throw them out," Dadu said.

"She's going to catch something," Ammu said. "Throw them out."

Abbu was silent. I loved the kittens, so I would catch something. Fantastic!

Three kittens, white, black-and-white, red-and-white, surrounded the mother kitten. Like the sweetest of tigers, they pounced on the paper balls I threw at them. Could anything else pounce so beautifully? Imagine throwing out such kittens.

"Don't throw them out," I told Ammu sadly.

"I'll get sick if they stay," Ammu said.

So, it was decided that the kittens would be thrown out.

Abbu told his brother, whom I called Kaku, "Throw the kittens out today."

But Kaku didn't do any work at home. He showed up, ate, played with me, called me funny names, hoisted me on his shoulder and danced, and then went out again. He would never bother to throw the kittens out.

"Haven't you thrown them out yet?" Abbu asked.

"I'll do it one of these days," Kaku said.

"It's got to be done today," said Abbu. "Have you seen how she holds them in her arms?"

Everyone was afraid that I'd catch something serious.

Illness was much closer to our home now.

"I'll have to do it myself," Abbu said.

Abbu gazed at the kittens. I brought him pieces of paper. But Abbu didn't make balls out of them to toss at the kittens as before. The kittens circled Abbu and me.

Abbu wrote, *How hard it was for me to throw the kittens out!*

Abbu never wrote in his diary about the fairies he took me to see one afternoon. He wrote about the kittens.

Putting the mother and the baby kittens in a sack, Abbu went out.

He hailed a rickshaw. The driver asked, "Which way, *saar*?"

"Any way you like," said Abbu, hauling the sack onto the rickshaw.

Evening had fallen. The city was sparkling with darkness and light. There was a nip in the air. Abbu sat on the rickshaw.

"Where to, saar?" asked the rickshaw driver.

"Take me to the park," Abbu said.

A little later, Abbu said, "I have to do something bad, you know."

"Bad, saar?"

"I'm throwing out our kittens," Abbu said. "I feel awful about it."

"You're bound to feel awful if you're throwing out pets," the driver said.

The rickshaw stopped on the eastern side of the park. The driver said, "Throw them away here, saar."

Abbu did not speak. The rickshaw began moving again. Eventually, the park was left behind.

"We've left it behind, saar, the place to throw them away."

"Oh," said Abbu. "Turn around."

The rickshaw turned back.

On the eastern side of the park, where the road was as beautiful as the floor of a house, where the walking track was even lovelier, where there was a green carpet of grass,

Abbu loosened the mouth of the sack holding the kittens and left it on the ground.

As soon as he started walking, the mother and two of the babies jumped out of the sack. The third one was stuck inside. Abbu had almost reached the rickshaw by then. He went back to release the kitten. As soon as it was free, the kitten jumped out to join its mother, brother, and sister. They were mewing. A kitten leaped in the air. The mother jumped onto the wall. The babies tried too. It was too high for them. The mother jumped down.

Abbu took his seat in the rickshaw. It started moving. Abbu had tears in his eyes. The rickshaw traveled a long way.

"Let's go back to the kittens," Abbu told the driver.

"Are you feeling very sad, saar?" the driver asked.

The rickshaw went back. The mother kitten was walking with her babies. They were northward bound. One of the kittens was walking ahead. The mother was in the middle. The other two babies were behind her. They seemed to be leaving the park to go back home.

Where will they go? Abbu asked himself. Abbu did not know.

Abbu came back home. He did not speak. I climbed onto his lap. He didn't dance with me. He didn't laugh with me. Abbu went out again after a short while.

I went back to the park, Abbu wrote. *I thought I'd find them on the road. I wanted to bring them back. I looked for them a long time. But the cat and her babies were nowhere to be seen. My glasses had misted over.*

Speak, Photograph

How fine it would be if photographs could talk, if photographs could walk. I have a pile of black-and-white photographs.

The age of color had not dawned yet. Every photo I own is black and white. Some of them have faded. But nothing in them can escape my eye. I can even see the things that have vanished. The photos are collected in a handful of small albums like gold. They have things written on the back in Abbu's hand. Beautiful handwriting, like beads of pearl. If only my handwriting were that good!

I really do look like a fool in one of the photographs. I've stuck a pen in my mouth. That's the photograph. I'm chewing a pen. Apparently, childhood is the time to try to eat everything. Is this pen a good one? Chew a corner to find out. Is that brick of high quality? Lick it to be sure. Is the book a masterpiece? Chew the cover and see what it's like. How will you know what things taste like unless you chew them?

I'm sitting in Abbu's lap, chewing a pen.

Abbu seems to be saying, "Must you chew everything?"

I seem to be saying, "How else will I know what the pen is like?"

Abbu seems to be saying, "What else do you wish you could chew?"

I seem to be saying, "I wish I could chew the moon to find out why it's so white."

Abbu seems to be saying, "What else dost thou wish to consume, thou genius, thou fool?"

I seem to be saying, "I wish I could chew the sun to find out why it's so red."

I like looking at Abbu's photographs. It seems as if Abbu has emerged from the photographs to stand in front of me. And that he has started talking to me. In many of Abbu's photographs, his eyes are almost shut, as though Abbu were asleep—even though he is sitting or standing or holding me in his lap or putting his arms around me.

"Why do you fall asleep during photographs, Abbu?" I ask.

"I'm afraid of the camera," Abbu seems to say.

"Why do you curl your lips that way?" I ask.

"I'm trying to smile," Abbu seems to say.

Abbu's hair covered his forehead. His ears too. The part on the right-hand side was so sharp. He wore glasses with thick black frames. Would the frames have been as thick today?

"Why are your frames so thick, Abbu?"

"So that I look like a professor," Abbu seems to say.

"Would you have worn such thick frames now?"

"No, I would have worn golden frames now," Abbu seems to say.

In one photograph, I'm walking in the park, holding Ammu's hand. In another, I'm sitting on the branch of a tree.

Everyone is silly in childhood, and the photographs are even sillier. Mine are absolutely ridiculous. But some of them are lovely. I want to kiss myself in them.

"Why aren't all photographs beautiful?" I ask Abbu.

Abbu might say, "Photographs of beautiful people are always beautiful. Other people's photographs are beautiful sometimes."

"Why do you part your hair on the right, Abbu?" I ask.

"For fear of Baba," Abbu says. "My father wouldn't even allow me to comb my hair. A part on the left would have meant trouble."

"But I part my hair on the left," I say.

"Because your abbu is not my abbu," Abbu says with a smile.

Abbu goes back into the album when I shut it. Our conversation stops. As soon as I open the album, Abbu walks around the room, onto the balcony, across the green grass in the park. He leads me by the hand, clasps me to his breast with kisses, calls me "genius, fool."

I gaze at Abbu. I see Abbu, and I don't see him.

Twenty-Four Hours in My Life

A crib had been made for me. Before I became me, I used to sleep in it like a kitten. How soft it was. How beautiful the patterns on its sides were. There was even a white mosquito net. I used to sleep and sleep and sleep in it, with a bottle in my mouth. But as soon as I became me, as soon as I learned to stand on my own, no one could make me stay in the crib.

The patterns felt like a prison. Getting to my feet, I would cry, "Oh oh gnn gnn." Abbu would run to pick me up in his arms. Ammu would run to pick me up in her arms. What joy in escaping those bars!

I refused to be put back in the crib.

"We paid so much for it," said Ammu.

"It's just taking up room now," said Abbu.

The horrible crib was removed. I was so happy. Who wanted to sleep alone in that cold crib when I could sleep in Ammu's arms with one leg on Abbu's tummy?

They found out straightaway that I was a firecracker. I'd go to bed next to Ammu, and dip and skip up on Abbu's other side. Sometimes a leg on Ammu's face, my head nestling on Abbu's chest. If you have to sleep, that's the way to do it. Am I a rock that remains still? It's all right to be that way if you don't have dreams, like rocks don't have dreams. But I dream all night, and in my dream, I wander about in the land of the fairies. That's why I spin all over the bed.

No one understands this. Can those who never dream understand those who do?

Ammu forces me to lie down on the rubber sheet.

Ammu gets angry in her sleep. "Stay there."

Why shouldn't she be angry? Ammu hasn't had a full night's sleep since my arrival.

That rubber sheet? Ugh! Someone makes sure it's wet all night. Can someone who dreams possibly sleep on a rubber sheet?

I have lots to do, so I'm the first to wake up. Even before Ammu. I play with Ammu's hair when I wake up.

I tug at her locks to find out to whom they belong. And whether they're strong.

"Don't pull," says Ammu. "It'll come out."

I stick a finger in Abbu's nose. I didn't want to put my finger in his nose. I wanted to grab his face.

Waking up with a sneeze, Abbu hugs me and bites my cheek.

Ammu runs to the bathroom as soon as she's up. She has to rush. Ammu puts on her sari hurriedly. Why does Ammu wear such a beautiful sari so early in the morning? Why doesn't she dress me in new clothes?

One day, I realize Ammu turns into a fairy when she puts on a beautiful sari every morning. She goes off somewhere. No matter how much I go, "Oi, oi," she doesn't respond. Ammu doesn't stay at home once she's turned into a fairy. She goes off somewhere. When Ammu puts on her new sari, I see she has grown two lovely, colorful wings. Ammu uses those wings to fly far away.

But I'm a match for her. As soon as she puts on her sari, I jump into her arms.

"Go to Fazila now," Ammu says.

I have learned to shake my head. "Naah naah oi oi," I say.

Ammu has to carry me to the top of the stairs. I jump into Fazila's arms. Ammu turns into a fairy and goes off somewhere.

Abbu is very nice. He doesn't get dressed so quickly. When he goes into the bathroom, so do I.

What does Abbu put on his face? What's that white thing Abbu puts on his face? Abbu is such fun.

The instrument goes *cring-cring*, *cring-cring*. I get excited.

I waddle toward it. Abbu is busy with his face. I run and fall on my face. The *cring-cring* stops. I cry.

It's been put high up because of me. Although I run toward it when it goes *cring-cring*, I can't reach it.

My eyes are fixed on the door. Where does everyone go through it? Where does everyone come from through it? One day, the door is open. As soon as I set one foot outside, I fall. But I grab the railing. Abbu comes running.

"What a boy!" Abbu says. "Can grab the banister already."

"He's a rogue, a rogue," says Ammu, taking me in her arms.

I walk along the balcony in a dress. I'm going to peep into Abbu's study. The moment he sees me, Abbu jumps up from his chair and comes to me.

"Catch, catch," says Abbu.

I run off slowly. Abbu runs as though he can't catch up. He trails behind. I run into Ammu's arms.

I've learned many words. One of the sweet ones is "naughty."

"Do you know how naughty I am, Abbu?" I ask Abbu.

"How naughty?" says Abbu.

"At nap time, I just close my eyes; I don't nap," I tell Abbu.

"Then who naps in the afternoon?" says Abbu.

"I do," I say, jumping in the air.

It's so much fun when Abbu brings chocolate. Abbu doesn't hand it over at once. That's what makes the chocolate sweeter. That's what makes me want the chocolate even more.

Abbu asks from the door, "Where are you?"

I shout, "H . . . e . . . r . . . e . . ."

Abbu says again, "Wh . . . e . . . re?"

I say, "H . . . e . . . r . . . e . . ."

Abbu says, "Who wants chocolate?"

He holds the chocolate high in the air.

I put my arms around Abbu, dancing with joy. "I do, I do, I do."

Abbu breaks off a piece of chocolate and puts it in my mouth. How sweet the chocolate tastes.

Walking Barefoot at Dawn

Abbu tells me all the time to put on shoes. Who wants to wear shoes so much? Abbu's eyes are always fixed on my feet.

All that Abbu says is, "Where are your shoes, where are your shoes, where are your shoes?"

It deafens me. My feet hurt from all this wearing of shoes. What I like is to walk barefoot on the floor. To get my feet wet, my face wet, my clothes wet in the bathroom. How sweet the cold was that night. I was so toasty under the quilt with Ammu, in the warmth of her body. It was almost dawn, and I wasn't awake yet. Abbu was awake. How strange, Abbu woke up even before me.

Abbu poked me. "Wilt thou come?"

My sleep was like a china cup. It could be shattered at the touch of a fingertip.

"I will," I said, opening my eyes.

I jumped up.

"What's this, you want to take her too?" asked Ammu.

"Hmm," said Abbu.

I'd slept enough. I leaped out of bed. Abbu dressed me. I ran to get my shoes.

"No need for shoes today," Abbu said.

I was so pleased. I wanted to sing, *No shoes today, no shoes today.* Abbu hadn't put on his shoes either.

"Go ahead. I'll join you afterward," said Ammu.

When we went out, how wonderful, there were so many people, none of them with shoes on their feet. Not on my feet, not on Abbu's feet. Not on the feet of the man in front of me. Or the man behind me. Everyone was walking slowly. They were singing like they were crying, the way I cry sometimes like I'm singing.

Many of them had flowers. Some of them had large garlands.

Everyone was singing like they were crying softly. Everyone was crying for their brother. Had so many people lost their brother on the same day? Could a day become red with the blood of everyone's brothers? The brothers of so many people? Who was he? Who were they, all these lost brothers? I didn't have any brothers. I was nobody's brother. Who were they, these brothers of all these people?

"Sing," said Abbu.

So Abbu could sing? I had never heard Abbu sing before.

Abbu was singing, "My brother's blood has turned it red, the twenty-first of February, it's a date I'll never forget . . ."

Was Abbu's brother lost as well? And Abbu couldn't forget him either?

I sang too, "My brother's blood . . ."

Who were these brothers whom everyone had lost and so was forced to cry for as they walked barefoot at dawn? I felt like crying when I sang, "It's a date I'll never forget." It was so crowded here. Where were we going? I couldn't keep up with the crowd, so we walked along the edge of the road. How magnificent they looked as they marched in rows. Their singing made my heart tremble.

Abbu brought some flowers from somewhere. He pinned a black ribbon on my chest. I had a black ribbon on my chest and flowers in my hand.

What was this day that had dawned? We had never had a day like this before, a day of so many people, of so many flowers, of black ribbons, of singing for our brothers. Or perhaps we had, but I was too small for Abbu to have brought me.

A girl came up to us and picked me up in her arms.

"Goodness," she said, "how you've grown. How does it feel to be here?"

"I feel like crying," I told her.

"No, don't cry," she told me.

She was dressed in a black sari. So were many others. We were walking. But do you think it was easy? There were people and more people. All of them singing like they were crying. I kept wishing we could go much farther.

I couldn't walk anymore. I had never walked so much. My feet felt funny. But I was happy. Abbu picked me up in his arms and walked for a long time.

Then I saw everyone laying the flowers in front of a sun. A mountain of flowers. Soon they would cover the sun. The scarlet sun would sink into blue flowers. Everyone was lining up to lay flowers.

We, Abbu and I, moved forward slowly toward the sun. *It's a date I'll never forget,* I sang in my head, and laid my flowers at the foot of the sun.

Abbu put his flowers at the foot of the sun. It seemed to me the sun was turning into a huge flower and filling up everything, and the flowers were turning into red suns and spreading everywhere.

When we returned home, I cried in my heart. It's a date I'll never forget . . .

The Birth of a Flag

Abbu wrote, *I expected something like this. "Pakistan" is another word for "betrayal." Nothing happens there without conspiracy and treachery. The election is a farce. They thought they would be able to crush the Bengalis by calling for an election. They thought the Bengalis wouldn't get a majority, and the Pakistanis would retain control. That the sacred land of Pakistan would remain under the army generals' boots.*

Abbu's diary entries had grown quite long by this time. Earlier, I used to be on every page, but ever since we walked barefoot to lay flowers at the feet of the sun, my presence in Abbu's diary had shrunk. The nation, the language, and Bengalis had grown prominent.

Bengalis dream of ruling Pakistan, Abbu wrote. *What an impossible dream. That day will never come. Why has Pakistan amassed so many weapons? Their armed forces are experts at occupying their own country. They will wipe out all Bengalis if need be, but they won't let them come to power. Pakistan's people can never hope to live in a democratic country. It's impossible to have military rule and democracy at the same time.*

This was the kind of thing Abbu wrote. I couldn't understand any of it when I read it in third or fourth grade. But today I understand it very well. I look around me, and I know.

Abbu and Ammu came home early that day. I was thrilled.

"Dangerous times ahead," Abbu told Ammu.

"I think so too," Ammu said.

I was always frightened to hear of danger. I had been in danger one day when my foot got caught between the bed and the wall.

"Why danger, Abbu?" I asked. "Is it because you came home early?"

Abbu took me in his arms. "No, there's no danger because we're home early. We're home early because there's danger."

I could see for myself there was danger when Abbu took me out to the balcony in his arms.

The same people who had been on the streets barefoot a few days ago were out again today. But they weren't weeping and singing, "I can never forget." They were angry.

"J-o-y B-a-n-g-l-a!" they were shouting together. "Victory to Bangla!"

This time, they were not without their shoes. They weren't carrying flowers. They didn't have tears in their eyes and a tune on their lips. They were pumping their fists in the air. Some were carrying sticks. They were rushing somewhere. They were shouting, "Victory to Bangla."

"Victory to Bangla," Abbu whispered.

I loved it. Raising my arm, I shouted, "Victory to Bangla."

The parade was unending. One stream of people was followed by another.

Their screams rent the sky. "Victory to Bangla."

I ran around the house, shouting, "Victory to Bangla."

Abbu's diary was full of Bangla, Bengalis, and liberation. Abbu wrote:

March 1, 1971

The students rushed to the university in groups as soon as the announcement was made on the radio. I went out of the classroom. We were told the national council would not have its session in Dhaka. It was completely out of the blue. Our hearts sank. Our heads were in turmoil. There was fear too. What were the Pakistani demons about to do? ("Demon" and "human" were among Abbu's favorite words. Abbu hated demons. He considered the rulers, the Pakistani overlords and their generals, nothing but demons.) *They were bound to attack the Bengalis.*

There was an avalanche of people on the streets. A sea of faces. A single cry all around us: "Victory to Bangla!" It made your nerves tingle. Your temperature shot up when you added your voice. People were taking over the streets of the second capital. On Jinnah Avenue, in Tejgaon, everywhere. Parades were converging on Dhanmondi from every part of the city.

March 2, 1971

All of Bangla has shut down. Offices are closed, schools are closed, colleges are closed, the university has turned into a fortress. Only the streets are flowing. Torrents of people. Bangla has never seen so many processions. We are moving toward our destiny. But will autonomy be enough now, or do we need something larger, like independence? But can independence come so easily? Does it not need blood, unending blood?

Pakistan has been burned to ashes today at the University of Dhaka. We were buried under the crescent and star all this time. We Bengalis. It's the flag of treachery. It will not do for us anymore. We need a new flag, as the students and student leaders of the University of Dhaka showed us today. Some of them may lose their way in the future, but today they have set an example for all Bengalis.

The top of the western gate of the Faculty of Arts has become immortal today. There we were, thousands of us, standing in front of the building. A sea of people. The student leaders climbed on the top of the gate, delivered their speeches, and then set fire to the crescent and star.

The green flag, "our community flag," went up in flames. The Pakistani national anthem, "Pak Sar Zameen Shaad Baad," was burning. The moon burst into flames, and the star followed. Pakistan was burned to ashes.

A new flag was born in its place, entirely green, with a bright red sun in the center, and on it, the contours of Bangla, all fifty-six thousand square feet of it. I felt my heart was fluttering there on top of the gate of the Faculty of Arts in the form of that flag.

The flag was flying, the flag was flying, our new flag was flying, our new flag was flying all over Bangladesh.

Suddenly, a wave of fear spread over us. There was a rumor that the Pakistani military was on its way, that it would demolish the Faculty of Arts, where the crescent and star flag had been burned. They would drench the place in the blood of the students, the blood of the people. We began to run. I set off homeward . . .

Late in the afternoon, a flag began to flutter on our roof. I had never seen a flag before. It was a green flag, dark green. A sun in the middle, just like the sun at whose foot I had laid flowers that day we walked barefoot. There was something drawn inside the sun.

"What's this, Abbu?" I asked.

"This is Bangla, Bangladesh," said Abbu. "Our country."

Our flag was flying on our roof. Bangladesh was fluttering on our roof. Closing my eyes, I saw, on this roof and that roof, on those roofs, roofs, roofs, the flag, the flag, the flag. Bangladesh was flying, Bangladesh was fluttering. In my heart, on the roof.

March Is the Cruelest Month

Abbu wrote, *Revolution comes to our land along with spring in February. Winter recedes, old leaves fall. New foliage and flowers pierce the bone-dry branches to be born. Rebellion arrives, and with it, revolution.*

I began to be happier from the day the flag was flown. Ammu no longer turned into a fairy and left every morning. Whenever I climbed into Abbu's arms on the balcony, I could see people and more people. I don't think I have ever seen so many humans together since then. And the shouts, "Victory to Bangla!"

Abbu's diary was filling up with acts of revolution. Abbu wrote:

March 3, 1971

Thousands of people with sticks and rods are marching from every direction toward Road No. 32 in Dhanmondi, with earsplitting cries of "Victory to Bangla." But will they receive wise counsel there, or will the rebellion of millions falter? I do not think it will fail. Bengalis have grown as fearless as tigers. Mobs have surrounded the Pakistani military in Tejgaon. They are attacking the army in Sylhet. They are battling soldiers in Kumilla. Fires are raging everywhere. All that remains is for everything to be burned down.

Maulana Bhashani held a meeting in Paltan today, stoking the flames burning within everyone. Our veteran leader has hinted at independence. But the center of all attention today is No. 32. People will come back in a few days from No. 32 with either success or failure.

March 7, 1971

An enormous platform has been erected at the racecourse. All the leaders are gathered there. The Ramna Racecourse is the Bay of Bengal today, with all the rivers of Bangla flowing into it. There are roaring voices all around. Processions are arriving from every direction. Students are streaming in from schools and colleges and universities. Laborers are marching from Adamjee and Demra, from Tejgaon and Tongi. The leather workers are here, the garment workers are here, the peasants are here. Victory to Bangla. Victory to Bangla. Victory to Bangla.

The same cry reverberates from one parade to the next. Will the army attack us? A helicopter flies overhead. We are frightened. Then we overcome our fear. Everyone is saying the Pakistani military has turned into a toothless tiger. Is this true?

What is this roar that Sheikh Mujibur Rahman has just let out? All of Bangladesh is in his heart today. It is the collective war cry of Bangla that has come from him, spreading out over the racecourse to the public library, to the Faculty of Arts, to the High Court, to Ramna Park, before crossing the river and Tongi to travel everywhere, across the entire land. Schools are closed. Colleges are closed. Universities are closed. Banks are closed. Offices are closed. And if even a single shot is fired . . .

Sheikh Mujib's warning to Pakistan fires us up. Will he announce our independence today? Our hearts are in turmoil. Will he prove revolutionary enough to make the declaration right now? The public is ready for it. They will rush to Tejgaon the moment it is made, just as they did in '69. Sheikh Mujib says, "This battle is for freedom. This war is our liberation war." It scares me.

This is not exactly a declaration of independence, then. The word "liberation" confuses us. There are different kinds of liberation, but there can be only one independence.

But his call to war echoes in our breasts as we come away from the meeting fearfully. "Turn every home into a fortress,"

*he says. "Turn every home into a fortress. This war is our lib-
eration war. We will free the people, God willing." How will
Sheikh Mujib free us? Will we win independence from Pakistan
and liberation too? Or does Pakistan still live within him? Are
the students imposing a new flag on him, a new country, the
country of Bangladesh, and the song that sends our blood racing, "Amar shonar Bangla, aami tomay bhalobashi. We love
you, our dearest Bangla"?*

March 10, 1971

*Anyone who looks at Bangla today will see the world's young-
est, most intense flag. The revolutionary flag is flying fearlessly.
On the streets, there are nothing but flowing rivers of people.
They have sticks and rods; they have armed themselves with
whatever they could find. Their singing rings in our ears: "We
love you, our dearest Bangla." And there's the constant war cry,
"Victory to Bangla." There has never been such a time in the
lives of Bengalis.*

*What is Sheikh Mujib doing? Everyone is looking to him.
Which way is he leading us? Are we on the road to independence? If so, it will be a road strewn with blood and death.
There's no trusting the Pakistani army, even if they're behaving
like toothless tigers now. They are bound to spring on us sooner
or later. Does Mujib realize this? Do the students, the laborers,
the peasants realize this? How will we combat them in our*

homes? Can rifles and cannons and tanks made in China and America be confronted with sticks and rods?

We will be Pakistan no more. It's time to be Bangladesh.

March 15, 1971

What conversations has Sheikh Mujib had with Yahya Khan, with Zulfiqar Ali Bhutto? Does he trust them? That can only lead to calamity. Does Sheikh Mujib still dream of becoming the prime minister of Pakistan? Do East Pakistan and West Pakistan still seem a single country to him? If so, grave danger lies ahead. He must show us a clear path. But they say he is holding secret talks with representatives of the army. Is he himself in the dark? Will he, too, find out Pakistan's intentions in the most violent way, like the rest of us? They want to drink the blood of Bengalis; they want to snuff out the lives of Bengalis. Does Mujib not understand this? Perhaps he doesn't, because the politics he believes in cannot bring independence to a nation—it only elevates one's own party and political class to the seat of power.

March 20, 1971

A lot of blood has been shed in Bangladesh this March. In Chittagong, in Tongi, in Jessore, in Khulna, in Sylhet. The Chittagong port has been loaded with Pakistani arms. Sheikh

Mujib does not understand, or perhaps he does not wish to understand, what Yahya and Bhutto want to achieve while pretending to have a dialogue with him. He thinks the demons will bow to the will of the people. Demons never do that.

The people have their blood, and the demons have their weapons. It is weapons that triumph in this world. How is Sheikh Mujib unable to understand this, so unable to understand this, so completely unable to understand this? How long will unarmed citizens stand up to cannons, rifles, and tanks? Is Mujib going to make all of Bangladesh confront the armed demons without any weapons of its own?

Even the ordinary people have realized by now that talks will lead nowhere. Why does the leader not get it? How is he still laboring under an illusion?

March 23, 1971

It became obvious today that Pakistan is finished here. March 23 used to be Pakistan Day. The flag of Pakistan was unfurled in schools and colleges, in the yards of government buildings, and on the roofs of people's homes. But the Pakistani flag did not fly anywhere this year except in the army camps.

Today, it is the flag of Bangladesh that flew all over the land, along with black flags to signal grief. The sky of Bangla is a very different one today.

The day was observed as Resistance Day. The National Council was supposed to have met today, but that has been canceled yet again. The people and the army are clashing everywhere. What is Sheikh Mujib still discussing with the demons? Attempts are underway to disarm the Bengali soldiers in the military camps, so that they cannot mutiny. But the Bengali soldiers at the Joydebpur royal palace have refused to surrender their weapons. The signs of war are in the air.

March 25, 1971

The days seem to pass in futility. Mujib is revealing nothing about his interminable discussions. The people do not know what they should do. Is Mujib prepared for war? A journalist friend has brought terrible news. Apparently, talks have broken down. Yahya is supposed to have left for Pakistan in secret. Perhaps Mujib doesn't know. Yahya has left behind the ferocious Tikka Khan, who considers human blood an aperitif.

I spent the day meeting with people around the city with my journalist friend. Everyone wants to know what's going on. All of them have urgent questions, but no one has the answers. The answer that we all know is too abhorrent to be uttered. It spells blood. It spells war. My friend said we should go back home at night. Something may happen tonight. What is this something? Can we even imagine what it might be? At nine, I set off for Azimpur. When I arrived at the road to our house, I found the boys putting up barricades.

"Why the barricades?" I asked.

"The military may come tonight," one of the boys who knew me answered.

"Can this barricade stop tanks?" I asked lightly.

"No," he said, "but what else can we do?"

Are we about to go to battle unarmed? Will we turn into another Biafra? I am at a loss for an answer.

Gigantic rocks threaten to pulverize the heart of Bangla today. Countless weapons are aimed at it.

Night of the Demons

I cannot stay up late. So, I fell asleep. Loud noises woke me. I shouted. I clutched Abbu. Explosions everywhere. *Ratatatatat. Bambambam. Goomgoomgoom.* Screams from the east. And the sounds. *Ratatatatat. Bambambam. Goomgoomgoom.* Abbu switched off the lights quickly. The streetlights had gone out too. The lights next door as well.

"We'll sleep on the floor," Abbu told Ammu.

Ammu spread a sheet on the floor in the dark. I curled up on it, between Abbu and Ammu. I had my arms around Abbu. He was trembling. His palms were sweaty.

The sounds came again. Abbu made us crawl under the bed. At midnight, we had the bed above us. I couldn't sleep.

I was frozen with fear. How frightening the sounds were. *Ratatatatat. Bambambam.* Like a snake slithering in beneath the door, poised to strike.

"Water, Ammu." My throat was parched with fear.

The glass of water fell from Ammu's hands and shattered. It felt as though the *ratatatatat bambambam* had entered the room. Abbu leaped up.

"It's nothing," said Ammu. "I dropped the glass."

Every sound was terrifying. Even the snapping of a twig. I jumped in fear when someone opened a window. It all sounded like *ratatatatat bambambam.*

Which way were the demons coming from? Where were they shooting? I thought they had surrounded our house. They were firing their machine guns at us.

"The military must have come out of the cantonment," said Abbu.

"But why are they firing?" asked Ammu.

"The sounds are coming from the direction of the university."

"Are they killing people, or is it a threat?" asked Ammu.

"You heard the screams," said Abbu. "Pakistanis don't threaten; they just kill. They must have killed the students."

Abbu peeped out of the window. But the streets were not visible. It was not a night to see anything. It was a night to listen, and to collapse into the arms of a bloody death.

A shaft of flame was visible in the distance. It grew into a roaring fire. Even the darkness in our room was interrupted by sparks of light because of it.

Ratatatatat. Bambambam. Goomgoomgoom. Dawn had arrived. The call to prayers floated in from the mosque, shaking with fear.

We lay beneath the bed, against the wall.

"Stay here," said Abbu. "We won't get up now."

Ammu banged her head against the bed when she tried to sit up. She lay down again. I fell asleep. There had never been a more terrifying night.

The Flag, Again

"Take down the Bangladeshi flag from your roof," someone shouted from next door. "Fly the Pakistani flag instead."

I ran with Abbu to the balcony. We saw the crescent and star of Pakistan fluttering on all the roofs around us, where the flag of Bangladesh used to be.

Not a single red sun anywhere. Not a single outline of Bangla in the center of the sun.

"We've been ordered to fly the Pakistani flag," our neighbor said.

Abbu ran up to the roof to bring down the flag of Bangladesh. He was trembling uncontrollably.

"Where should I put this?" he asked.

No one knew. In our hearts, perhaps?

"Didn't we used to have a Pakistani flag?" Abbu asked.

"I have no idea," said Ammu.

She searched everywhere. Under the bed, in the kitchen, in the dustbin. The crescent-and-star flag was finally found in the trash. But it wasn't a flag anymore; it was a filthy rag. Both Abbu and Kaku had used it to clean their shoes. Fazila had wiped the floor with it. It was ruined. How could it be put up on the roof? The crescent was shredded, and the star had fallen off altogether.

"Give me an old green sari," said Abbu.

Fazila found an old green sari. She found an old white cloth too.

A crescent-and-moon flag was made. It refused to fly. It drooped.

Abbu put it up on the roof. It dangled from the post, as though it would never fly. Kaku spat on it.

The flag of Pakistan hung on our roof like a gob of spit.

Dhaka Is Fleeing

Abbu wrote, *There's a curfew all over town. I can no longer tell what's happening. There's a plume of smoke over Zahurul Hall. It's been rising since the morning. Did the military set the place on fire? Dhaka seems to be petrified.*

For the first time, we were confined to our room We didn't dare go out to the balcony. A strange silence everywhere.

Abbu wrote, *There's nothing but declarations of peace on the radio. I feel like throwing the blasted thing away. Just yesterday it was playing "Amar Shonar Bangla." What are these sounds coming out of it now? Where is Sheikh Mujib? What of all his discussions? What will happen now?*

Abbu wrote, *We trembled with fear when we heard on the radio this afternoon. First, "Amar Shonar Bangla" was played, and then came the announcement: "A civil war has broken out in East Pakistan." Then the song was played again, followed by the same announcement. I clutched the radio and trembled.*

Afternoon came, then evening, then night. And once again the *ratatatatat bambambam goomgoomgoom*. The second night of the demons began in our Dhaka. Ammu had already made our bed beneath the bed. We lay down there. Abbu could not sleep; Ammu could not sleep. Even I could not sleep. All I could hear was the sound just outside our door. *Ratatatatat. Bambambam.*

Abbu wrote:

March 27, 1971 (Entry on March 29, 1971)

The curfew was lifted in the morning. I went out for a look around the city. I never imagined Dhaka could have changed so much in just two nights. There were people everywhere once again, but while before they'd been dressed in clean, ironed clothes, now they seemed to have come out in their pajamas. Everyone's hair was disheveled, and they had dark circles under their eyes.

Walking through Azimpur to the Newmarket crossing, I was frightened by what I saw. One armored car after another zoomed past, their guns aimed at the people on the street. They seemed ready to fire. I was terrified before I had taken even a dozen steps. What if the rain of bullets began again?

All of Dhaka seemed to be fleeing. People were running away in rickshaws, on foot. Babies in their arms, children on their shoulders, bundles on their backs. Everyone's spine seemed bent. The people looked broken. The people looked defeated. None of them could hold their head high. They were cowering in terror, shriveled beneath their burdens. Barely a shop was open. The non-Bengalis who live here were driving around, shouting, "Long live Pakistan." Bent and broken, Dhaka was running away from Dhaka with the military all around.

The slums on either side of the railway tracks had been burned to ashes. Corpses lay everywhere. No one could look at them. The military's armored cars were right on our heels.

Corpses lined the floor of Zahurul Hall. Both the first and second floors were rivers of blood. I couldn't bear to look at the scene. Someone said it was worse in Jagannath Hall. G. C. Deb's body was lying on one side. I couldn't look. I couldn't move. I set off homeward. On the main road, I saw the armored cars behind me, their guns pointing at the people. Each one of those vehicles looked like a wolf with bullet wounds.

When I reached the house, I found everyone standing at the gate.

"Let's go," I said.

Instead of entering the house, we all set off for our village.

We're Going to Our Village

We were going to our village. I was very happy. I'd never been to our village. Nor had Abbu in a long time, or he would have taken me. What was a village like? Was it like in the picture?

Abbu picked me up in his arms. Dadu had hired someone to escort us to the village. He was carrying our luggage. Ammu was carrying my bag. Kaku was carrying a large case.

Abbu was carrying me.

Many others were on their way, just like us. We went up to the river along an old road. It looked like a road poor people lived on. People were crossing the river in boats.

Boats everywhere. People everywhere. Nobody was crossing over to our side of the river.

Why were we going to the village now? Why hadn't we been before? Was it because we couldn't sleep at night anymore? Were we going to the village because we were no longer sleeping in our beds? Had Abbu and Ammu decided to go on a vacation after all this time? I didn't know.

I was happy we were going to our village.

All of Dhaka was going to the villages. Had everyone been sleeping beneath their beds like we had? Was this a city that slept beneath the bed? Was this a city that couldn't sleep because of the *ratatatat* and the *boomboomboom*? There was a crowd of people on the riverbank. Everyone was leaving. No one was staying. I was very happy.

Some people came to receive us as soon as the boat was moored on the other side. They looked happy. Village people were nice. I was happy. One of them gave me a kiss.

Was this a village? There were trees everywhere.

Abbu wrote, *It was evening by the time we reached Jinjira. We would have to spend the night there.*

This was my first visit to the village. This was the first time I would stay in a village.

The place was filled with people. They had spread sheets on the ground to sit on, to lie on. By the houses, beneath the trees. Did you have to sleep beneath trees at night if you lived in a village?

Someone had recognized Abbu. So, we were taken into a house. Here in the village, we slept all night.

We didn't have to sleep under the bed here. But we could hear the *ratatatat* and the *boomboomboom* on the other side of the river, far away. A beam of light fell on this side of the river. It came from the other side.

In the morning, we began walking. I enjoyed the walk. It was a lot like walking barefoot that other morning. A pond here, cows there, houses nearby. I loved the village. The people of the village were very nice too. They had set up shops along the way.

"Have a cold drink," they said.

We had cold drinks. They didn't accept money from Abbu. They didn't accept money from anyone.

"What do you think will happen now, saar?" someone asked Abbu.

"War," said Abbu. "There's no other option."

What did war mean? I wondered.

The man who had asked the question carried me on his shoulders a long way. How nice everyone was. All the village people had smiles on their faces. Those who had come from Dhaka were finding it difficult to walk. Abbu walked a long way with me on his shoulders.

I walked a long way. Dadu walked a long way. Ammu walked a long way. We traveled a long way on a boat. Then we walked again. Only cold drinks on the way.

Kaku was carrying the radio. Suddenly, he shouted, "Independence, we're going to get independence."

What did independence mean? I wondered.

Everyone gathered around the radio.

Abbu wrote, *The sound seemed to come from a distance. Yet it also seemed close by. "This is Major Zia, this is Major Zia." Major Zia announced independence. An electric current ran through my body. My blood tingled. I felt we had got freedom.*

"What is independence?" I asked Abbu from his shoulders.

"Something very rare," Abbu said.

"What does it look like?" I asked.

"Like the red sun you saw," Abbu said.

One day, I had walked barefoot and seen a red sun. On several days, I had seen a sun on a flag. I remembered the sun.

"When will we get independence, Abbu?" I asked.

"No one knows," said Abbu.

I really wanted to know when we'd get independence. Abbu knew everything. Why didn't he know this?

I was aching all over from being carried and from walking. Ammu couldn't walk properly anymore. Abbu couldn't either. None of the people who were with us could walk anymore. It was evening, but we were still walking. So many people were walking. Many of them had left the road to walk in the fields. Maybe they were nearly home. In the morning, I'd been so happy to go to our village, but my happiness had dried up.

"Who knows when we'll go back to Dhaka," said Ammu.

"We haven't even left Dhaka properly yet," said Abbu.

Fear had gotten into my heart now. Everyone was saying Dhaka had become a dangerous place.

I thought demons had entered Dhaka. Their footsteps were making the *ratatatat boomboomboom* noises. We had left Dhaka out of fear of demons. When would we go back? Demons never died easily in all the stories I'd heard about them. They died eventually, but not easily.

My heart trembled with fear.

It was almost night. Everything looked sleepy. The trees looked like they would go to sleep any moment.

"There, that's the roof of our house," said Abbu.

Abbu showed me a house through the trees. It felt as though the house were falling asleep, just like me.

Tonight, my eyes would be full of sleep in a room full of sleep.

Green All Around

How lovely my village was! Green all around. Ponds every-where. How beautiful the earth looked! How clear the water in the ponds!

Many people came to see us. We went to see many people.

Abbu and Kaku waded into the pond to catch us some fish. I loved it. The crowd on the wide road running past our house just wouldn't stop. An endless stream of people kept walking by, coming from the same direction that we had. An endless stream of people.

The stands offering cold drinks had packed up. Everyone coming from Dhaka looked stricken with fear.

Whenever anyone asked how things were in the city, they said, "Very bad," and continued on their way.

I was sitting by the road with Abbu in the afternoon. All I could hear was "very bad." I didn't want to hear it anymore. Abbu no longer smiled like he used to.

Abbu wrote, *The villages are filling with people. Those who have not been home in years are flocking to their villages. They've come from Dhaka, from Narayanganj, from Jessore, from Chittagong, from Dinajpur, from Kumilla. They've come from everywhere. Every town is in the same situation as Dhaka.*

The army is shooting people, abducting people, setting people on fire. The cities are uninhabitable. Everyone has fled. But how long can we stay here? Will the military not come to the villages? We need money to survive. Where's the money?

The liberation war has begun. But liberation is a long way away. We cannot hide in the villages till then. There is nowhere to hide here. The villages will become the centers of the liberation war. The villages will be the capital of the freedom fighters. How should I take part in this war?

Those who came to visit Abbu had very bright eyes. They were full of hope. I sat by Abbu's side, listening to them. Their hope gave me hope.

Some said, "The military is in deep trouble. The freedom fighters are giving them a beating."

Some said, "We will be independent in a month or two."

Some said, "We have to build a liberation army here too."

Abbu said, "But we cannot expect to return to Dhaka soon. That's the military headquarters."

Some said, "It won't take long to drive the Pakistanis out of Dhaka."

"How will we do that?" Abbu wanted to know.

"The war," said everyone.

Abbu said, "But the war hasn't even begun properly."

Abbu wrote, *The war will have to spread everywhere. Only when it extends across the country can we be sure that victory will be ours. Everything that comes before that is just to keep our enthusiasm alive.*

We gathered around the radio as soon as it grew dark. Everyone did, and so did I, sitting next to Abbu. My heart danced to hear that the Pakistan military was suffering defeats everywhere. The others were as delighted as I was.

But no one knew when we could go back to Dhaka. Abbu didn't know; and nor did Ammu. The people who came to see Abbu didn't know either. I realized that the village didn't seem as green as it did before. It looked dirty now. The water in the ponds was not as clear as when we arrived. People didn't pick me up in their arms happily like they used to. I wished I could go back to my old Dhaka.

Abbu said, "Many non-Bengalis have joined hands with the military in Dhaka. Some Bengalis too."

"The non-Bengalis were bound to join them," Ammu said.

"Bengalis are being butchered in Mirpur and Mohammadpur," Abbu said.

"But how could Bengalis join them?" asked Ammu.

"Opportunists exist everywhere," Abbu said. "There are many traitors now. They are conspiring with the Pakistan army."

Conversations like these gave me nightmares. Dhaka was filled with demons. They were rushing toward our village. They had enormous teeth and nails. Screaming in fear, I threw myself on Abbu and Ammu.

I saw the green all around us turning filthy.

The Demons Are Coming

All I heard was "the military, the military."

"The military's coming," everyone said.

I'd never seen the military. Whenever I heard the word, I thought of demons. I had heard of different kinds of demons. I had dreamed of different kinds of demons. Enormous teeth, enormous claws. Huge tongues. Whenever I heard the word "military," I thought demons were on their way from Dhaka.

The Pakistanis were demons. Their soldiers were demons. They were approaching along the same road we had taken out of Dhaka. People were fleeing. Abbu and

Ammu were fleeing. But where could we escape to from the village? We couldn't escape.

It felt as though the military were marching along the road running past our house, as though they were marching through the lake on the other side. My blood froze with fear.

"The military is going into the villages," Abbu said.

"Where will we go, then?" asked Ammu.

"There's nowhere to go," said Abbu.

Ammu quaked in fear. So did I.

Every evening, Abbu and I would visit our neighbors. The only topic of conversation was the military.

An old man was passing with a cow.

"I hear the military's coming," he told Abbu.

"Sooner or later they will," Abbu told him.

The man was frightened. "Then where should I go?"

"There's nowhere to go," Abbu said. "We have to stay in the village."

Fearfully, the man took the cow toward the field. I was afraid for him. What if the military came from that direction?

Dadu talked about the military all the time. Dadi, my grandmother, had never seen the military, but she talked about it too. Fazila talked about the military. The girl who worked in the house we were staying in had never been to Dhaka. She talked about the military all the time too. None of them had seen the military. I hadn't either. But I had seen demons. I had seen different kinds of demons in my sleep.

I passed the days in fear of the military marching like demons along the road running past our house. The grayish village visible across the lake looked to me like a military platoon. They were approaching our village, our pond, our house. I stared at the grayish village, which seemed to be advancing toward us. The military was coming. How did they travel? Did they march or drive or fly? I knew nothing. So, it seemed as though the military was coming, their feet pounding the earth, with sounds of *ratatatat* and *boomboomboom*.

Dadu thought so too. Dadi thought so too. The neighbors whose houses I visited with Abbu thought so too. The cowherds in the fields thought so too. They no longer sang in carefree voices when they took their cows out to graze.

The stream of people walking along the road running past our house had not stopped. People kept coming. They kept coming. No one stopped them to offer cold drinks. They came on foot, rested beneath the trees, drank water from the pond, and continued on foot.

One day, a friend of Abbu's arrived. Abbu was delighted to see him. Abbu's friend had never come to this house of ours. All he knew was the name of Abbu's village. He was going to Barishal. But he was staying at Rarikhal in Bikrampur now.

"Everything has gone awry," Abbu's friend said. "I have to take a roundabout route to Barishal."

"Ah, that's how you came to be here," Abbu said.

"All the towns are in bad shape," said the friend. "The military is going into the villages now."

"What should we do?" said Abbu.

"I'll probably cross over to the other side," Abbu's friend said. "That's why I'm going to visit my mother first."

Abbu and Abbu's friend looked worried. I began to wonder where the other side was. What if Abbu also crossed over to the other side? Where would we live? Would we also cross over to the other side? How far was the other side? I began to feel frightened. I wanted to cry.

"Will Abbu cross over to the other side, Ammu?" I asked her.

Ammu was startled. "Is he saying he will?" she asked fearfully.

"No, Abbu's friend says he'll cross over to the other side," I said.

Ammu was alarmed.

"Where's the other side, Ammu?" I asked.

"India," Ammu answered. "Different country."

What if Abbu went off to a different country? How would I live? Where would I live? How would I live without Abbu?

Where was this country? How would Abbu go there? Was there no military there? When would he come back? Would we go too? Would Ammu go? Would I go? I felt frightened to think of another country and the military. Every tree in the distance looked like the military to me.

"Will the military come here?" I asked Abbu.

"Are you very frightened?" Abbu asked me, picking me up in his arms.

"Hmm," I said.

Abbu held me close and gave me many kisses.

"Don't be frightened," he said.

"Aren't you frightened?" I asked.

Abbu gazed at me for a long time.

The people who visited Abbu every evening came today as well. They no longer had smiles on their faces.

"A military vessel passed along the river today," they said.

"Which way did it go?" asked Abbu.

"Westward," they said.

Everyone looked worried. Darkness had fallen. I felt the military was approaching us along the road running past our house. I clung to Abbu.

Another Night of Demons

The entire village quaked in fear that evening. People began to stream toward our village from Borobazar, the market near the village across the lake, beyond which was the Padma River. Everyone said the military had landed on the bank of the river that afternoon. They were approaching the other village. People were fleeing. Some had entered our village.

Others were going farther instead of stopping here. They weren't walking, like we had walked from Dhaka. They were running. "The military is here, the military is here," they screamed. "They have come ashore from the river."

Abbu turned pale.

"Where do we go now? Where do we go?" moaned Dadu.

Ammu picked me up in her arms.

Abbu went out on the road with many others, to find out what had happened. When he came back, he said it was true. The military had entered the market. The people had fled in fear. Both the market and the village had been emptied out. I didn't know how far our village was from the river. I began to think of the road running past our house as the river. And the house next door as the market the military had entered.

Many people came to talk things over with Abbu. What to do, where to go, where to flee.

"Aren't there a lot of Hindu families in that village?" someone asked Abbu.

"Almost everyone in that village is Hindu," said another.

"Where are they now?" asked Abbu.

"They're still in the village," someone else replied.

"They must be told to run away," Abbu said.

"Muslims are in danger too," said someone.

"Everyone is in danger," said Abbu, "but Hindus are in greater danger. That's why they must be informed."

"I'll go," said someone.

He left on his bicycle.

Darkness fell. No lights went on in our house. No lights went on anywhere in the village. We had already finished dinner. Everyone was trembling in fear, just like me. A little later, the *ratatatat boomboomboom* began from the village by the river. We could see a big fire.

Our village was lit up by the flames. *Ratatatat boomboomboooom. Ratatatat boomboomboooom. Ratatatat boomboomboom.* Screams floated across from the village by the river. Everyone in our village ran into the jungle near our house.

We had to cross a pond to enter the jungle. I had seen the jungle from a distance. Abbu was carrying me. We went into the jungle on a boat. People from everywhere had come into the jungle. There was nothing but people around us. We sat down under a tree. I was frozen with fear. The fire in the village by the river had lit up the jungle too.

We could hear the sounds. *Ratatatat boomboomboom.*

We were holding one another. Abbu was holding me. Ammu was holding me. Dadu was holding me. The sounds wouldn't stop. Screams kept floating in from the village by the river.

No one was talking. I had so much to say. I was holding it all in my heart. But I didn't say a word to Abbu. Ammu didn't say a word to me either. Every time there was a sound, they held me tighter. I held them tighter.

I could see the demons out in the village by the river. They had enormous teeth and claws. Their eyes emitted flames that set the trees on fire, set the houses on fire. Tongues of fire rose into the sky. I squeezed my eyes shut in fear. Were the demons approaching our jungle?

They seemed to be threatening Abbu with their claws. They seemed to be threatening Ammu with their claws. They seemed to be threatening the entire village with their claws.

Abbu wrote, *The military set the village on fire that night. They shot people all night. Many people died, over a hundred. More would have died if they had not fled. Most of the dead were Hindus, though some Muslims died too. But the military had come to torch the homes of the Hindus. They were well informed. This is what is happening everywhere. Almost all the homes of the Hindus have burned down. The village is like a crematorium now. How beautiful it was once upon a time.*

Abbu wrote, *The village by the river was burned to ashes. The military did not enter our village. But there's no guarantee that they won't in the future. Every village and every town and every city is within reach of their bullets and their torches. Our village isn't safe anymore. How long can we live this way? I feel like crossing over to the other side. I'll have to leave them behind. Should I leave them behind in the village, or in Dhaka? Dhaka is safer than the village now. There's no option but war. We have to go to war.*

To the Burned-Down City

"It's best to go back to Dhaka now," said Dadu.

He had been to Dhaka a few days before. He went to our home. We were frantic with worry. He was supposed to have stayed there for two days. Everyone started crying when he didn't return as planned. But Dadu came back from Dhaka on the third day. A wave of happiness ran through the house.

"The city is filled with the military," Dadu said.

"Aren't people frightened?" asked Ammu.

"There's not as much fear now," said Dadu. "People are moving about even though the military is everywhere."

"Then we can go back to Dhaka?" asked Ammu.

"I'm not sure," said Dadu. "But things are better than before."

"Are Bengalis moving about on the streets?" Abbu asked.

"They are," said Dadu. "But with caution. There are rumors everywhere."

"What rumors?" asked Abbu.

"That the military is being defeated by the liberation army," said Dadu.

So, we would go back to Dhaka? The mere mention of the military made me afraid. Still, we set off for Dhaka. This time, we didn't have to walk the whole way. We walked part of the way and boarded a small launch. Bengalis supporting the military, who were called *rajakars*, searched our luggage. Then we took a bus to Jinjira, the village where we had spent a night. But the village wasn't like before. It looked different.

There were rajakars again when we crossed the river. There were rajakars when we went ashore on the other side. "All rajakars," said Abbu.

They seemed just like us. They spoke Bangla. Why were they on the side of the military, then? Why did they search our luggage so often?

"They're bad people," said Abbu. "They've joined hands with the military. There are people like them in every country, people who find joy in taking their brothers' lives."

I began to hate rajakars.

We rode back home on rickshaws along those roads that had looked like poor people lived on them. Everything had changed. Everywhere there was silence. Everyone was afraid, but they weren't going to flee anymore. This was not the city we used to live in. Dhaka had burned down and become a different city.

I realized how different as soon as evening fell. I was sitting with Abbu and Ammu. The doors and windows were shut. Abbu was trying to tune in to the radio broadcast. Suddenly, there was a sound. "Boom!" We were plunged into darkness.

"There, listen," said Abbu.

"What was that sound?" asked Ammu.

"Can't you tell why it's dark?" said Abbu.

"No," said Ammu.

"The liberation army has blown up a power station," said Abbu.

Abbu seemed happy when he said this. So I was happy too.

"Look, Dhaka has changed," Abbu said.

Abbu had new clothes made after our return to Dhaka. For himself, and for me too. Abbu had never worn clothes made of this kind of fabric. Nor had I. It was striped, hand spun. I loved the colors.

"You're wearing handloom clothes," said Ammu in surprise.

"Everyone is nowadays," said Abbu.

My new shirt had a strange smell.

"Dhaka has changed, you know," said Abbu. "Its clothes have changed by day; its activities have changed by night."

When darkness fell, we waited for the bombs. I didn't like it till I heard the explosions. I hated it. Then I loved it the most when we heard a bomb bursting in the distance and the lights went out. We could hear military vehicles on the road. If only someone would drop a bomb on them!

A Broken Sun

One day, Abbu took me out to see the city. We were dressed in our new clothes. We had to walk a long way before getting into a rickshaw.

Before, the rickshaws would be lined up near our home. Not anymore. There were very few of them on the roads now. Very few people. A military car went past our rickshaw. I had never seen the military before. I was seeing it for the first time now.

"That's a military car," Abbu whispered to me.

So, this was the military? The soldiers looked even worse than demons.

Demons didn't glare all the time. They didn't hold guns ready to fire. The Pakistanis were even worse than demons.

What route did our rickshaw take? I didn't recognize it. It was so silent, so desolate.

"This is the university," said Abbu.

"The university, the university, the university," said I.

"The military have killed many people here," Abbu said. "The students used to live over there, but they don't anymore. Many of them have been murdered."

I'd been to my aunts' homes with Abbu. I'd met the fairies one afternoon with Abbu. The city used to look different then. Not like it did now. So few people. So few cars. So few rickshaws. So few people. So few cars.

"There used to be a large banyan tree there," said Abbu.

The tree was gone. Students used to have meetings beneath it. So the military cut down the tree.

"There used to be a temple here," said Abbu.

A temple, where Hindus used to pray. The military had killed the Hindus. They had demolished the temple.

"There used to be a slum here," said Abbu.

The slum was gone. The poor used to live here. The military had killed them. No slum. No people. Another military car passed us.

Another one. Our rickshaw kept moving. Another one. Our rickshaw kept moving. Another military car passed us. Our rickshaw kept moving. Another military car passed us. Our rickshaw kept moving. Another military car passed us.

Our rickshaw kept moving. Another military car passed us. Our rickshaw kept moving . . .

I had been here once. At dawn. With thousands of others, barefoot. Everyone was singing a sad song. There were flowers everywhere. There were countless bouquets. A red sun was shining here, at whose foot I had laid flowers. Abbu had laid flowers. Everyone had laid flowers. Where was the sun now? Where was the tower? Razed to the ground. It was lying in pieces. The tower that was smothered in flowers. *My brother's blood has turned it red, the twenty-first of February, it's a date I'll never forget.* Languishing in the dust now. We gazed at it from the rickshaw. Passersby averted their eyes. Looking at it too long made you want to cry.

Another rickshaw passed us. The man in it looked at us and suddenly started singing, "We love you, our dearest Bangla." Abbu jumped in surprise. He trembled. I trembled.

It had been such a long time since I'd heard the song. No one around us sang it anymore. There was a time I'd hear it every day. "Our dearest Bangla." The other man's song shook us. It shook the city under the control of the military.

Those Handsome People

They would visit us at home one by one, not in groups. How handsome they were. They would hug me. They would greet Ammu with sweets. They would greet Abbu. When people visited us before, Abbu would sit with them in the living room. There would be tea and cookies. There would be conversation and laughter. They would hug me and kiss me. After our return to Dhaka, there were no more conversations in the living room. Whenever anyone came, Abbu took them into the bedroom. They talked in low voices. Everything had changed. The days of talking in low voices were here. And of peeping through the window from time to time.

The conversations did not last long anymore. The visitors would come, say something to Abbu in low voices, and leave. Some of them would come again. Once again, they would talk in low voices and leave. They came every day.

Abbu went out every morning. He returned in the afternoon and sat in silence for some time. There were visitors afterward. Abbu went out in the evening, and came back late at night. I was asleep by then.

Abbu never used to come home as late as he did now. Abbu had changed too. He peeped through the window often. He never used to peep through the window.

"Do you know there's a war on?" Abbu would tell me.

"What's a war, Abbu?" I'd ask.

"Fighting," Abbu would say.

Abbu and his friends were in a war against the military. Abbu and Kaku and the rest of them. I was frightened. The military was uglier than demons. Abbu and Kaku and their friends were so handsome. Was it right for the handsome to fight against the ugly? Could the handsome ever win against the ugly? Could the ugly ever win against the handsome?

Sometimes Abbu would hold me very close. He would give me kisses. Abbu used to talk a lot. Now he didn't talk much. He only liked to hold me close. I would also hold him close with my eyes shut.

Ammu talked less too. Ammu had begun turning into a fairy again and going out every morning. But Abbu had no fixed time for going out. Abbu was never quiet. Abbu had loved bouncing me in his arms. He didn't bounce me in his arms anymore.

One afternoon, Abbu told Ammu, "I'm not coming home tonight. Eat and go to bed on time."

Abbu had never spent the night out of the house. Why would he do it tonight?

"I'll tell you later," Abbu told me.

Abbu never told me later.

Did he tell Ammu? What did he tell my ammu?

Abbu didn't come home that night.

But someone knocked on the door very late that night. I was lying with my arms around Ammu. I couldn't sleep because I couldn't stop thinking of Abbu. Where was Abbu now? Why hadn't he come home? Ammu jumped out of bed. So did I.

Dadu woke up too. People were banging on the door now. They were kicking it.

"Who is it?" Dadu asked.

"The military," they said.

They were looking for Abbu. Ammu was about to collapse on the floor. I was trembling uncontrollably. I clung to Ammu and Dadu. They kept kicking the door. Dadu opened the door. The military came in. They began to look everywhere for Abbu. They asked where Abbu was. Dadu said he had gone to the village to fetch Dadi. The military and the people with them were looking at us cruelly. I was terrified. I kept saying to myself, *Thank goodness you're not at home, Abbu; thank goodness you're not at home, Abbu.*

Where are you today, Abbu?

The military left. Ammu sat with me in the living room.

Ammu wouldn't be able to sleep that night. I wouldn't be able to sleep that night. We could hear military vehicles outside.

Why wasn't Abbu home that night? Did Abbu know the military was coming? Would the military have taken Abbu away? Would they never have brought him back? Why did the military want to take my abbu away?

Abbu came back the next afternoon. I exploded with joy at seeing him. Ammu looked happy too. Abbu held me close for a long time. He looked at me for a long time. He ran his fingers through my hair. He and Ammu had a conversation.

"Go to sleep on time and eat properly every day," Abbu told me.

"All right," I said.

"I won't be back for a long time," Abbu said.

I clung to Abbu. He left soon afterward. All of us went downstairs. Ammu was weeping. I was weeping. Dadu couldn't even go downstairs. Abbu handed me over to Ammu and walked away slowly.

He turned and smiled at me before he rounded the corner.

Abbu's smile hung in my eyes like tears.

Where Are You, Abbu?

Abbu's smile hung in the air all around us. Wherever I looked, I saw Abbu's smile. Hanging in the air. But I couldn't see Abbu. Abbu was no longer at home. Abbu no longer carried me in his arms to the front door when we went out. Abbu no longer picked me up in his arms when he came home. I no longer had an abbu whose arms I could jump into. Abbu was no longer there to carry me on his shoulder.

Abbu, Abbu, I called out to him in my head, *come back. I hate it without you.*

I hated going to sleep because Abbu wasn't there. I hated eating because Abbu didn't give me kisses. I hated waking up because I wouldn't find Abbu lying next to me. All I did was stand on the balcony. All I wanted to do was lift the curtain and peep outside. I jumped up every time there was a knock at the door. I ran to see who it was. I hated my lunch because Abbu wasn't there. I wanted to throw up after drinking my milk because Abbu wasn't there. I didn't feel like putting on my clothes because Abbu wasn't there.

Where have you gone, Abbu? Where are you now, Abbu? When do you wake up in the morning, Abbu? Where do you sleep, Abbu? Why don't you come to me anymore, Abbu?

Why don't you take me in your arms and call me "fool" anymore, Abbu?

I remember those fairies. I wish I could go to them again with you. I wish I could see the blue fish with the fairies and with you. I wish I could go out at dawn with flowers. I wish I could sing the song that sounded like we were crying. I wish I could hold your hand and walk to the sun. I wish I could lay red flowers at its feet.

Where are you, Abbu? Why don't you come home anymore, Abbu?

You asked me to eat my meals, Abbu. I hate eating now.

You asked me to go to sleep on time, Abbu. I cannot sleep anymore; I cannot ever sleep.

I want to see you, Abbu. I want to see my abbu.

I want to see you, Abbu. I want to see my abbu. I want to see you, Abbu. I want to see my abbu.

I remember Abbu. I remember my abbu. My abbu, I remember him. I remember my abbu. My abbu, I remember him.

I want to see you, Abbu. I want to see my abbu. I want to see you, Abbu. I want to see my abbu.

Where are you, Abbu? Abbu, my abbu? Come home at once, Abbu; come at once. I cannot sleep. Ammu cannot sleep. I don't feel like eating. Ammu doesn't feel like eating. I sit quietly. Ammu sits quietly. Our house stands quietly. Our bed stands quietly. Your books stand quietly.

None of us can sleep because of you, Abbu.

Ammu and I

Ammu was just like me. She kept going out onto the balcony. She peeped through the window all the time. She jumped up every time there was a knock at the door. I was just like Ammu. I kept going out onto the balcony. I peeped through the window all the time. I jumped up every time there was a knock at the door. Dadu was just like me. He kept going out onto the balcony. He peeped through the window all the time. He jumped up every time there was a knock at the door. Ammu was just like me. She lay in bed but couldn't sleep. I was just like Ammu. I lay in bed but couldn't sleep.

"When will Abbu come, Ammu?" I asked.

Ammu was silent. After a long pause, she said, "He'll come."

"When?" That was all I asked.

Ammu was silent. After a long pause, she said, "He'll come."

"Where's Abbu gone?" I asked.

"To war," said Ammu. "Don't tell anyone."

Ammu fell silent again. I loved it when the bombs exploded at night. I felt it was Abbu's doing. It was his handsome friends' doing.

The bombs were killing the demons. They were killing the military, who passed loudly on the streets in their cars. Who had entered our home to take Abbu away. Who had broken the sun.

Abbu would come back after killing the demons. But so many days had passed now without his returning. I had stayed up for Abbu so many nights. Abbu wasn't back.

When would Abbu come? When would he and his friends kill all the demons? How long would I keep peeping through the window in search of Abbu?

Abbu didn't come. One of his friends came one day. I was so happy. He told us so many things about Abbu. Quietly. Holding me tight.

I didn't know how to read. But Abbu had written me a letter.

> *How are you? Are you eating and sleeping properly? Are you brushing your teeth? Are you listening to Ammu? I'm very well. I'll be back soon. It won't be long now. We'll go to the sun again. Lots of kisses.*
>
> *Abbu*
> *November 14, 1971*

I made Ammu read it to me hundreds of times. My only letter. A letter I stored in my heart like kisses.

A Constant Knocking on the Door

Then one day, the planes appeared in the sky. I thought they would form patterns. Such lovely milky-white planes! Many, many planes flew in. There was a lot of noise across the city. The sound of the military vehicles on the streets grew louder. I saw lots of planes from the balcony. As soon as they came, the skies would fill with bangs. "The war has begun," Ammu would say. At last the demons would be destroyed. We heard bombs all day and all night. I listened closely. And I imagined that, with each sound, Abbu had taken one more step toward home. I could see Abbu coming.

Abbu was smiling as he approached our house. It wouldn't be long before Abbu would be back.

Everyone seemed happy. After a long time, there was happiness on everyone's face. All of us crowded around the radio. But I alone could see Abbu coming home. How would Abbu be dressed? Had his hair grown very long? Would he be holding a gleaming rifle? I could see Abbu walking with his handsome companions along the road through the villages. One more plane had arrived in the sky. It looked like a fish. I liked it.

One day, there were celebrations in the streets. The military vehicles couldn't be heard. There was only one cry. "Victory to Bangla. Victory to Bangla. Joy Bangla."

Everyone was shouting, "Victory to Bangla."

Ammu looked happy. But she also looked strange. The cries could be heard all around us. "Victory to Bangla. Victory to Bangla." It was time for Abbu to be home.

Abbu would come home now. At last, the red sun could be seen on the green flag. Red in the middle, green all around—they were fluttering everywhere. One was flying on our roof. Another on the neighbor's roof. Another on the roof of the house across the street. Flags were fluttering on the street. Everywhere. Abbu was coming home.

I looked at Ammu. Ammu looked at me. Dadu looked at me. Abbu was coming home.

Independence was here. Why wasn't Abbu?

There was a knocking on the door. Someone was knocking again and again. I was sure Abbu was here. I was sitting when I thought I heard someone knock. I ran to the door. No one there. Ammu heard someone knocking. She jumped up to open the door. No one there.

As soon as I came back into the room, I heard the knocking again. There was no one when I went to the door. Ammu heard the knocking again. There was no one when she went to the door. Someone knocked on the door of our house all the time. There was a constant knocking on the door. All day long. All night long.

For a long time, the knocking on the door wouldn't let either Ammu or me sit still for a moment. For many months, I thought Abbu was knocking on the door. Abbu was calling my name. I could hear him clearly. There was no one when I went to the door. Only the sound of the knocking. From morning to afternoon, from evening to nightfall, then all through the night. A constant knocking on the door. The sound of Abbu's knocking on the door. There was no one when I went to the door.

"We hear all this knocking on the door, Ammu," I shouted. "Still Abbu doesn't come. Why not?"

"The knocking will go on forever, but your abbu will never come home." Ammu burst into tears.

"Abbu, Abbu," I screamed.

I remember Abbu. I don't remember Abbu.

Photo © Masud Hossain

Humayun Azad (1947–2004) is regarded as one of the most influential writers in modern Bengali literature in Bangladesh. An esteemed poet, academic scholar, critic, and linguist with more than seventy titles to his credit, Azad produced an oeuvre that is both rich and multidimensional. He was awarded the Bangla Academy Award in 1986 for his contributions to Bengali linguistics. In 2012, the government of Bangladesh honored him posthumously with the Ekushey Padak Award. Throughout his career, he was praised for his outspoken critique of fundamentalism and his unflinching support of the Bengali language and the culture it represents.

Born in Rarikhal, Dhaka, in 1947, Azad had his early education at Sir J. C. Bose Institution, Rarikhal, and higher studies at Dhaka College and the University of Dhaka. He earned his BA and MA in Bengali, standing first in the class in 1967 and 1968, and obtained his PhD in 1976 from the University of Edinburgh. He taught at the University of Chittagong and Jahangirnagar University and was a professor of Bengali at the University of Dhaka. On August 12, 2004, Azad died in Munich, Germany. He was laid to rest in Rarikhal, his rural homeland.

ABOUT THE TRANSLATOR

Arunava Sinha translates classic, modern, and contemporary Bengali fiction and nonfiction from Bangladesh and India into English. More than forty of his translations have been published in India, the United Kingdom, and the United States. Twice he has earned India's top translation prize, the Crossword Book Award for translated books. He was born and raised in Kolkata and lives and writes in New Delhi, India.